WE CAN READ!™

Molly's Store

by Jacqueline Sweeney

photography by G. K. & Vikki Hart
photo illustration by Blind Mice Studio

BENCHMARK BOOKS

MARSHALL CAVENDISH
NEW YORK

For Gabby, my Molly, and
Kristin, my Ladybug

With special thanks to Daria Murphy, reading specialist
and principal of Scotchtown Elementary, Goshen, New York,
for reading this manuscript with care and for writing the
"We Can Read and Learn" activity guide.

Benchmark Books
Marshall Cavendish Corporation
99 White Plains Road
Tarrytown, New York 10591

Text copyright © 2001 by Jacqueline Sweeney
Photo illustrations copyright © 2001 by G. K. & Vikki Hart
and Mark & Kendra Empey

Library of Congress Cataloging-in-Publication Data
Sweeney, Jacqueline.
Molly's Store / Jacqueline Sweeney.
p.   cm. — (We can read!)
Summary: Molly convinces her friends to set up a store in order to make enough
money to go see Quacker Jack and the Peeps.
ISBN 0-7614-1116-X
[1. Mice—Fiction. 2. Animals—Fiction. 2. Moneymaking projects—Fiction.]
I. Title II. Series: We can read! (Benchmark Books/Marshall Cavendish)
PZ7.S974255Mo   2001   [E]—dc21   99-056690   CIP   AC

Printed in Italy

1 3 5 6 4 2

Characters

Eddie

 Hildy

Ron

 Tim

Ladybug

 Gus

Molly

 Jim

Quacker Jack

 The Peeps

QUACKER JACK

& THE PEEPS
at Willow Pond

Quacker Jack!" yelled Eddie.
"He's coming!"
"He's coming to Willow Pond!"

"Quacker Jack and the Peeps?"
asked Ladybug.
She fluttered her wings.
"Yes!" said Eddie.

"No one sings like Jack!"

quacked Hildy.

She could not stop flapping.

"He's coming tonight," said Eddie,
"and I want to go."
"Me too!" cried Hildy.
"Me too!" cried Tim

"Let's all go," squeaked Molly.

"Costs money," said Jim.

Eddie groaned.

"How can we get money?"

"That's easy," said Molly,

"open a store."

She scooted away.

"Molly!" shouted Jim.

"Molly!" shouted Tim.

"Where are you?"

"Catch!" said Molly.

A button flew into the air.

Two white beads flew next—
then a shoelace,
three marbles,
a silver chain.

Ron hopped by.

"Here — catch!" shouted Molly.

"It's for our store."

Out flew a bottle cap,

two ribbons,

a stick of gum.

"Where did you get all this stuff?"
asked Gus.

"Picnics," said Molly.

"I get great food from picnics,"
grinned Eddie.

"I get great *stuff*," said Molly.

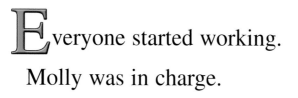

Everyone started working.
Molly was in charge.

"Jim, you juggle," she said.
"Hildy and Tim hold signs."
"Put more stuff on Gus!"
she shouted.

Molly's tove

Soon the store was open.

Porcupine bought popcorn.
Skunk bought shampoo.
The owls bought buttons
and a marble for Boo.

All day Molly shouted,
"Sale! Sale! Two for one!"

At last she cried,
"Store's closed!"

Ladybug started counting:
fourteen acorns,
sixteen seeds,
nineteen feathers,
ten tall reeds.

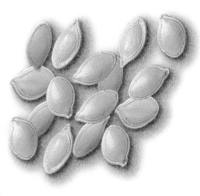

"Well?" asked Molly.

"Shhh!" said Ladybug.

"Add the two, carry the one."

"Yes," she said, "We made it!"

Everyone shouted, "Hooray!"

That night Quacker Jack and the Peeps
came to Willow Pond.

Hildy sang along.

Eddie and Ron stamped their feet.

And thanks to Molly's store,
they all had front row seats.

WE CAN READ AND LEARN

The following activities are designed to enhance literacy development. *Molly's Store* can help children to build skills in vocabulary, phonics, and creative writing; to explore self-awareness; and to make connections between literature and other subject areas such as science and math.

MOLLY'S CHALLENGE WORDS

There are many challenging words in this story. Choose one action word (a verb) and one person, place, or thing (a noun) from the list below. Ask children to use them together to create sentences.

air	bought	costs	fluttered
groaned	juggle	money	reeds
row	sale	scooted	shampoo
signs	store	stuff	

EASY FEET

Have children trace their feet on construction paper and cut out the shapes. Write long e words with ee or ea from the list below on each one. Put the "feet" in a line in random order. As they "walk the feet," have them read each word and use them to tell a story. (You can also use different feet like those of the animals in the story—webbed, clawed, etc.)

Long e words:

easy	beads	seats	seeds
reeds	peeps	feet	sixteen
nineteen	squeaked		

LADYBUG WORD WINGS

Cut red circles from construction paper and similar-sized circles from waxed paper. Cut the waxed paper in half and glue the halves on the red circles for Ladybug's wings. Now cut the red circles in half. Choose a compound word from the following list and write one part on each half. Have children match up the parts to create compound words. (They can be put together using paper clips.)

30

Ladybug   nineteen   shoelace
everyone   popcorn   sixteen
tonight

MOLLY'S STORE

Use items from around the house or classroom to create your own store.
Name your store and write advertisements for it. "Sell" items using play
money or small change. This is a great hands-on way to help children count
coins, make change, and learn the value of money.

PROBLEMS AT WILLOW POND

Using the objects from the story, create word problems to practice problem
solving and computation skills. For example, the owls bought two buttons
and one marble for Boo. How many items did the owls purchase at Molly's
Store? Have children write each problem on an index card along with a
drawing. Save them for practice!

NEIGHBORHOOD CONCERT

Give your very own concert, just like Quacker Jack and the Peeps! Have
children invite their friends to create a musical celebration.

Instruments might include:
> Combs covered with waxed paper
> Drums made from empty coffee cans and plastic lids
> Guitars made by stretching rubber bands across cardboard

About the author

Jacqueline Sweeney is a poet and children's author. She has worked with children and teachers for over twenty-five years implementing writing workshops in schools throughout the United States. She specializes in motivating reluctant writers and shares her creative teaching methods in numerous professional books for teachers. She lives in Stone Ridge, New York.

About the photo illustrations

The photo illustrations are the collaborative effort of photographers G. K. and Vikki Hart and Blind Mice Studio. Following Mark Empey's sketched storyboard, G. K. and Vikki Hart photograph each animal and element individually. The images are then scanned and manipulated, pixel by pixel, by Mark and Kendra Empey at Blind Mice Studio.

Each charming illustration may contain from 15 to 30 individual photographs.

All the animals that appear in this book were handled with love. They have been returned to or adopted by loving homes.